The Mermaid Who Came to School

You can take me home

First published 2008 by Macmillan Children's Books, London, in
'Mermaid Stories'

Published by Paperchard Books 2011

ISBN 978-0-9571099-0-2

This book is also available as an ebook,
a colour paperback, and an audiobook

The Mermaid Who Came to School

Written and Illustrated by

Moira Munro

Paperchard Books

When Leena was lonely she
practised walking on the bottom of the
sea. While her parents worked on their
oyster farm, she played at being a
human, swinging from side to side on
the very tip of her fish tail.

In the mornings, as soon as her
mum and dad had left to check the
oysters for pearls, she slipped away
towards the shore. She hid in the waves
that lapped against the sea wall, gazing

1

longingly at the little school just above.

'What I'd like to do,' she thought, watching the chattering children who gathered by the school gates, 'what I'd really like to do, is to get up on that jetty and join them.'

When she was little, Grandma had told her tales of mermaids making friends with humans. It was  rumoured that her great-great-aunt had run off, as a young mermaid, to marry a man. Dad snorted at these stories.

'Sea spray and nonsense! The terrible truth, Leena, is that humans are worse than sharks.'

Her parents had one rule, which they regularly reminded her of: never, ever let a human see you.

Yet there was one human Leena longed to be with. Every morning before school, this girl, who looked about Leena's age, skipped down to the beach for an early swim with her mother. Every time, the mother would say, 'Just a quick dip, Megan, OK? Or you'll be late for school again.' Megan

was a big smiler. Even when she shrieked that the water was freezing her toes, she never stopped smiling. What's more, she swam almost as well as a mermaid. Leena would dip and dive around her, quick as a mackerel so that Megan would not see her.

But last week, her father had caught her by the shore and sent her straight back into the deep.

'Are you mad, Leena?'

'But Dad, I have nothing to do all day long! Anyway, I'm really careful, honest!'

He'd ruffled her hair. 'I know it's lonely for you here, Leena. But this is where the farm is. I'm sorry. You stay close to us.'

All week, Leena had stayed away from the shore, but as she tossed in the  raging sea, the wind constantly whisked her mind off towards the little school.

Finally, one blustery morning, Leena could stand it no longer. With a determined flip of her tail, she sped

towards the shore. If she hurried, she would be in time to see the children coming into school.

She didn't expect to see the purple dragon in front of the gates. Nor the two giggling princesses, nor the alien chasing them into the school. For a wild moment, Leena wondered if she'd been sucked into one of Grandma's tales. Then she understood. A banner hung above the entrance, with the words WORLD BOOK DAY.

'That's it!' she thought. 'They're all dressed up as storybook characters.'

Megan arrived just as the bell was ringing. She wore a shimmery top, a sparkling necklace, and – Leena's heart skipped a beat – a glossy fishtail that went right down to her ankles. Leena danced a little jig in the sea. Of all the possible characters Megan could have picked, she'd chosen to be a mermaid.

An idea began to form in Leena's mind. It was a crazy idea. It was dangerous. If her parents ever found out, they'd never let her out of their

 7

sight again. She'd be stuck with them at the farm, twiddling her flipper while they tended the oysters, and they'd put her on pearl-stringing duties. And the real danger, of course, lay with the humans …

But, she thought with a leap of her heart, it's now or never.

Ten minutes later, Megan was walking through the school corridor with a message for the Head, her fishtail flapping around her ankles. Megan loved her costume. Often, in

the sea, she glimpsed flashes of
rainbow and fancied that a mysterious
mermaid was playing hide and seek
with her. Megan stretched her arms
forward and pressed her palms
together. She was gliding in the water
currents. She was leaping in the foam.
There, just beyond the corner, she
would join the biggest wave that—

THUMP!

Megan flung her arms
out to steady herself. Her
hands caught another pair of
hands. Delicate hands, cool and slightly

damp. Megan's eyes opened wide. The girl she'd bumped into was also dressed as a mermaid. How beautiful she was, with her big eyes and her sleek hair, so shiny she could have come straight out of the sea. And how her fish tail shimmered!

The two girls grinned at each other. Leena clung onto Megan's hands, trying to recover her balance. She may have practised for hours walking on the sea bed, but doing it on dry land was much more difficult.

Megan held her steady, laughing.

'These fish tails are terrible! I keep falling over as well. It's amazing how your tail completely hides your feet!'

Leena giggled. 'That's because mine's real!'

She clamped her hand to her mouth. Only a few minutes through the door, and already she'd said too much. 'Don't listen to me, I'm just pulling your fin.'

But Megan wasn't paying attention

anyway. 'Where did you get your costume?' she gushed. 'Mine's from Toy World. Your necklace is gorgeous. I bought one like that at the One Pound shop, but it's not so pearly.'

'Have it if you like,' Leena said, unclasping it from her neck. There were plenty more pearls at the farm. They were nothing special to her, nothing as special as a friend. Megan removed her own string of glass beads and hooked it round Leena's neck.

'You look lost – are you new? I'll

take you to the Head's office.'

Leena looked worried, suddenly.

'Don't worry, Miss Turner's not scary. She's going to be amazed when two mermaids turn up at her door!'

A big black dog leapt up from behind Miss Turner's desk the instant the girls entered the office. He growled and snapped at Leena's tail. Miss Turner jumped from her chair and yanked him away.

'Sit, Duke, *sit!*' she cried. 'What on

earth's the matter with you?'

'He thinks Leena's
costume is
dinner!'
Megan
joked.

Miss Turner shooed Duke into his
basket, apologising. But when she
realised that Leena had come in
without her parents, she folded her
arms and looked stern.

'Let me get this clear,' she said.
'Your parents just dropped you off?
Without coming to see me?'

Leena had been taught not to tell lies. 'I, er, came on my own, Miss Turner.'

'You walked from home, all by yourself?'

'Walked? Hmm … not exactly.' How could she tell the truth and still keep herself safe?

Miss Turner frowned. 'Where are your parents?'

That was an easy one to answer. 'They're busy on the farm.'

Miss Turner returned to her desk.

 15

She has a slight limp, Leena noticed.

'Listen,' Miss Turner said, more

gently this time,
'however busy your
parents are, they need
to come in right away, and
either register you properly or take you
home. What's their phone number?'

Leena's eyes searched the ceiling.
Foam number? What was that all
about?

Miss Turner continued. 'Leena,
where do you live?'

Leena pointed towards the window. 'The ocean. I mean, Ocean Avenue!'

'Ocean Avenue,' Miss Turner said. 'Hallelujah, we're getting somewhere. What number?'

Leena bit her lip. This was all getting harder than she'd imagined.

Miss Turner sank in her chair. 'So, no phone number, no address …'

For a while, the only sound was the drumming of her fingers on her desk.

Megan gave Leena's hand a little
squeeze.

Finally, Miss Turner stood up.

'Leena, let me look into this,' she
said. 'Meanwhile you'd better stay safely
with us.'

Leena beamed,
relieved. Megan led her
out of the office, saying, 'Don't worry.
Just get your parents to come over, and
then you can stay forever.'

Leena nodded. She wasn't worried
about 'forever'. All that mattered was

that today, on World Book Day, while everyone was dressed up, she would have a wonderful time pretending to be a human. A human dressed up as a mermaid.

If the Head hadn't guessed her secret, surely no one else would?

The children in Megan's class gazed, open-mouthed, at the beautiful new girl.

'I'm asking everyone to talk about their storybook character,' said the teacher, Mr Brown. 'Trandulah, it's your

turn. Why are you dressed up as a fairy?'

'So we can't see she's a witch!' shouted one of the boys.

Trandulah scowled at him. 'See my magic wand? When I wave it, everyone has to do what I say.'

'And if they don't,' a girl sniggered, 'Tell-Tale Trandulah will tell the teacher!'

The class giggled.

'That's enough, everyone,' Mr Brown

said. 'Now, would our two mermaids like to describe their characters?'

'Mermaids are beautiful and enchanting,' Megan began. Leena nodded enthusiastically, grinning.

'We're brilliant swimmers,' Megan added.

Leena agreed. 'We can glide through the wildest of seas.'

'And we're mysterious,' Megan continued. 'We sit on rocks with our sisters and comb our silken hair.'

'Not me,' Leena interrupted, rolling

her eyes. 'I don't have any sisters. There are no other mermaid children for miles, and no mermaid  school. I sit on my own at the bottom of the sea, getting bored out of my fish tail, while my mum and dad work on their oyster farm.'

Everyone laughed.

'But we don't mind having nothing to do,' Megan said, 'because we get to keep an eye out for handsome princes who need rescuing.'

Leena screwed up her nose. 'With

my luck, my prince would be uglier than a blobfish.'

The class burst into laughter again.

'For the sake of love,' Megan continued, 'we will gladly give up our enchanting voices, like *The Little Mermaid* did in the story. It's supposed to be a beautiful and brave thing to do.'

'I'd never be so stupid,' Leena said. 'What if after all that trouble, my prince picked his nose at the table? I

wouldn't even have a voice to yell at him!'

Mr Brown chuckled. 'All right, thank you, mermaids. Now, for those of you who'd like to perform in the school musical, Miss Turner and I will audition you now.'

Everyone sprang to their feet. Megan grasped Leena's arm. 'The school musical looks like brilliant fun. But only the best singers get in,' she whispered. 'I'm so nervous.'

Leena smiled. 'Don't be. Remember, you're a mermaid today. Mermaids have the most beautiful voices.' She nudged Megan. 'Unless they lose them for a daft prince!'

So, as Megan sang her audition piece, instead of worrying, she imagined she was a mermaid sitting on a rock, warming her face in the sunshine. Miss Turner and Mr Brown nodded at her. 'Well done! You're in,' they said, and everyone clapped.

But when it was Leena's turn to sing – a lilting, otherworldly melody – a

hush fell over the room. Never before
had anybody heard anything so pure, so
sweet, so perfect. When Leena stopped,
there was a long silence. Then
somebody clapped, and the class broke
out in cheers.

'Leena,' Miss Turner
said, wiping her eyes, 'that
was utterly enchanting. Are
you sure you're not a real
mermaid?'

Leena stiffened.

Behind her, Trandulah poked her
tail. 'Gross,' she hissed.

Megan led Leena away towards the dining hall. 'Ignore Trandulah. The main thing is, we're in the musical together. And we're best friends.'

Best friends. Leena felt warm all over.

A group of girls caught up with them as they joined the lunch queue. 'Hey, Leena. Love your costume.' One of them bumped into Leena, and she struggled to regain her balance on her fishtail. A dozen hands reached out to steady her.

'Either your costume is too tight,' Megan said, 'or you are mightily hungry!'

'Both!' Leena said.

Trandulah was ahead of them in the queue. 'Fish fingers,' she ordered.

Leena stared in horror. Her tail went weak and wobbly, forcing Megan to steady her again.

'Don't you like fish?' Megan asked.

'I do,' Leena said. 'They don't talk much, but they're

very friendly.'

Megan burst out laughing. 'Sounds like you'd better have the veggie dish.'

When the dinner lady held out her hand for money, Leena opened a small pearl bag and scooped out a handful of battered silver coins.

The dinner lady chuckled. 'I see you're a proper little mermaid! Let me guess: this is ancient treasure from the bottom of the sea, right? Fallen out of a sunken ship?'

Leena smiled politely through gritted teeth. What was she supposed to do now?

Megan pushed a coin into Leena's hand. What kind of parents did Leena have, she wondered, sending her to a new school alone, and not even giving her lunch money!

'Have it. I'm not that hungry myself.'

'We'll share,' Leena said, hugging her.

Trandulah swivelled round. 'We're

not allowed to give away our lunch money,' she whined. 'I'm going to tell Miss Turner. And stop laughing, you two, or you'll be in big trouble.'

Later, Mr Brown talked to them about the stars, some of which are so far away that the light coming from them has taken millions of years to travel to us. Leena wished she  could listen to him forever. Nobody, not even Grandma, had ever told her about stars. And nobody had ever asked her to perform in a musical and nobody had ever laughed with her and exchanged necklaces. As the last bell of the day rang, her heart sank to the bottom of her tail. This was it, then. Time to return to the sea.

She hadn't worked this bit out.

The bit where she'd have to say, 'Goodbye, and I loved being your best friend, and by the way, I'll not be coming back'.

A fierce wind was blowing in, and rain lashed Leena and Megan's faces as they made their way out of the front

door. Children barged past them to race down the steps, covering their heads with their school bags. 'See you tomorrow, Leena!' they yelled.

Miss Turner was standing outside, struggling with an umbrella. 'Leena,' she called. 'I couldn't get hold of your parents. Tell them to bring you in tomorrow, will you? We'll get you properly registered, and we'll sort out a school uniform for you as well.'

'It's OK, Miss Turner,' Leena said quickly. 'Goodbye.'

She rushed down the wheelchair ramp, her fingers gripping the wet handrail. She blinked back rain and tears. Megan ran after her, tripped on her fabric fish tail, and landed hard on her knees. 'Leena, wait for me!'

She found Leena sitting on a dripping bench by the sea wall.

She fingered the necklace Leena had given her, wondering what was going on. Why did Leena suddenly look so terribly sad?

She thought of Leena's strange coins, her horror over the fish fingers, her beautiful voice, and of course, the rainbow fishtail that mysteriously hid her feet. Suddenly, it all made sense.

'Of course!' she cried. 'You're a real mermaid!'

Leena looked up in alarm. A huge wave crashed below them, showering them with spray.

'You are coming back tomorrow, aren't you?' Megan shouted above the

 35

storm.

Leena swiped at her tail. 'The school uniform's hardly going to hide *this*.'

'Who cares!' Megan cried. 'Miss Turner won't mind. Our friends won't mind. Nobody's going to mind.'

Leena shook her head. 'Humans are dangerous – not you, of course, but other people. Mermaids never, ever come onto dry land. It's not like in stories! I only risked it today because everyone was dressed up.'

Megan glared at her. 'You're not

even trying.'

Leena took Megan's hand. 'I swim with you every morning, you know.'

'That's not good enough. I thought we were best friends.'

'We're mermaid sisters. In the sea.'

'I can't spend all my time in water!'

'You don't understand,' Leena cried. 'I can never, ever let humans know I'm a mermaid!'

'I heard that,' a shrill voice interrupted. Megan and Leena

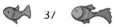

swivelled round to find Trandulah just behind them. 'You're half *fish*!' she shrieked.

Leena sprang up. 'I have to go!' Her tail slipped on the wet concrete and Megan grabbed her arm.

'Stay, Leena, please! Trandulah, get lost!'

Trandulah skipped round the bench and plonked herself on the edge of the sea wall. 'Hey everyone,' she shouted, waving her wand high in the air, 'freak show over here!'

'Get off the wall, Trandulah!' warned Megan.

'Let me go!' Leena shouted, trying to prise Megan's fingers off her arm.

Trandulah snorted. 'Ha! You're trapped. I'll tell the cook so she can turn you into fish fingers!'

Trandulah's mother charged towards them, arms outstretched.

TRANDULAH!' she yelled. 'Come away from the edge!'

Trandulah ignored her. 'I'll tell Miss Turner,' she shouted, throwing her hands up in the air. 'She'll have a fit when she finds out a sea creature was in her school.'

'TRANDULAH!!'
Megan and Leena leapt
forward, but it was too late. Trandulah overbalanced and fell backwards over the edge of the wall. Trandulah's mother screamed as a huge wave carried her daughter away, further and

further out to sea. For a few seconds there was chaos. Parents, children, Miss Turner, were screaming all at once. Some people wanted to jump into the raging waters, while others held them back.

The next instant, everyone gasped as a girl with a rainbow fish tail leapt off the wall. They watched her glide smoothly through the wild sea towards Trandulah.

'Who's that?'

'She's rescuing Trandulah!'

'She looks like a mermaid.'

'She *is* a mermaid. Look!'

'It's Leena! Leena's a mermaid.'

It took Leena only a
few minutes to return
the spluttering
Trandulah to the jetty. A great cheer
rose from the crowd. Trandulah buried
herself in her mother's arms and burst
into tears.

Miss Turner held her hands out to
Leena. 'Why didn't you tell me,' she
cried, holding Leena tight. 'Did you

think I'd turn you away?'

The children crowded around Leena, hugging her. Trandulah's mother ran over and planted a kiss on her cheek, before rushing away with her shivering daughter. A rumble of thunder reminded the parents that they too, should go home and get dry.

'I should go as well. Goodbye, Leena,' Miss Turner said, pushing her dripping hair away from her eyes. 'I'll get you registered tomorrow.'

'I can't …' Leena spluttered. 'My parents won't ever …' The storm

drowned her voice out, but Miss Turner understood.

'Ask them to meet me. I'll come here myself tomorrow, at sunrise. I'll come to the water's edge.'

'But Miss Turner, you're ...' How could she say this politely? ' ... not a mermaid, and my mum and dad would never trust—'

'I know,' Miss Turner said.

She bent down and tugged at the zip on her boot. Leena and Megan watched her, puzzled. Hopping

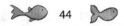

on one leg, Miss Turner pulled her boot off, and then her sock.

Instead of a big toe, Miss Turner had a small, rainbow-coloured fin.

'Wow!' said Leena.

'Amazing!' said Megan.

Miss Turner grinned. 'Tell your parents that my great-great-grandmother lived at Ocean Avenue too!' Then she put her sock on and zipped up her boot, and hurried back to the school gates.

Megan clapped her hands. 'Problem

 45

solved. She's practically a member of your family.'

'What's Dad going to say to that!' breathed Leena.

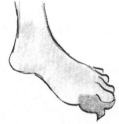

'Whatever he says, Miss Turner never takes no for an answer.'

Leena laughed. 'Then you'll definitely see me in school tomorrow!'

Megan threw herself forward to hug her, and Leena lost her balance and they tumbled, shrieking, into a puddle, but as they were both wet anyway, it

just made them laugh even more.

'You know something?' Megan said. 'I'm glad you rescued Trandulah. It was horrible when she fell in. Even though she usually is a pain.'

'I really didn't want to jump in,' Leena said. 'Not with everyone watching.'

'You risked everything for a human being – if you can call Trandulah that. Like the Little Mermaid did for her Prince.'

'Ahem,' grinned Leena. 'There is

one very big difference.'

'Oh yes?' Megan said. 'And what might that be?'

'The difference, mermaid sister, is that rescuing Trandulah is one thing ...'

'Whereas?'

'Whereas rescuing a prince is pure soppy.'

ABOUT THE AUTHOR

I went to schools where not a single mermaid was ever seen. Paris and Brussels are miles from the sea, so the chances of a sighting were pretty low. I now live in Glasgow, which is probably still too far for a mermaid to walk.

But I often visit children with my stories and illustrations, so perhaps one day, in a school or

library near the sea, I'll get lucky. But I'll be just as lucky if you, the reader, are transported to a rich other world every time you read this story.

You can find out more about my books, illustrations and school visits on www.moiramunro.com, where you'll also find the audiobook for this story, and pictures of various attempts I made at painting the cover. And if Facebook, Twitter and Google+ have become old hat by the time you read this, I'm sure my website will give you the latest way to be in touch.

 51

THANK YOU

The first version of this story was published in 'Mermaid Tales' by Macmillan Children's Books, edited by Emma Young. 'The Mermaid Who Came to School' was one of several stories by other authors, including Philip Ardagh, Jane Ray, Anna Wilson, and Fiona Dunbar.

Big gratitude to Emma Young and to Kathryn Ross for their editing of that first version.

ALSO BY MOIRA MUNRO

Hamish, The Bear who Found his Child

Written and illustrated by Moira Munro

Publisher: Piccadilly Press, London, 2003

ISBN: 1 85340 767 4

Hamish Bear lived in a teddy bear shop. It looked like a normal shop, with all the teddies arranged in rows on the shelves. But really it was a magical shop. When it closed at night, Hamish and his friends went through a secret door into their very own house - the

House of Teddies.

Although all the bears knew there was one special child for each teddy, Hamish didn't want a special child. He liked to do his own thing, and he especially liked to ride his scooter. But one day...

Discover the story behind the story
of Hamish on Moira Munro's website
www.moiramunro.com

Review by Anne Johnstone, The Herald

At first glance the lives of most of the children and creatures that appear here are fairly humdrum. However, the genius of clever, thoughtful picture books like these is their ability to expose in a brief sequence of text and images, the powerful currents of emotion that run beneath the surface.

As we close the covers, we can still feel the deep desperation of Hamish the teddy ... to find love and companionship. Sure, they're visual feasts, packed with fun and frolic but they're so much more.

As Francis Spufford argues in The Child That Books Built, stories can bring a child into a new relation to ideas because of the way they're crafted. Through books, he says, children experience differently flavoured lives to their own and it changes the way they think.

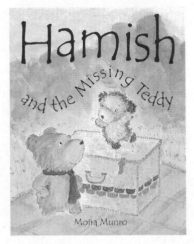

Hamish and the Missing Teddy

Written and illustrated by
Moira Munro

Publisher: Piccadilly Press,
London, 2004

ISBN: 1 85340 800 X

Hamish was off to the Great Teddy Bear Picnic with his small friend Finn. He waved goodbye to his special little girl. 'It's her birthday today,' he told Finn. 'As her special bear, I want to take a terrific present back to her.'

But all Finn wants to do is play with Hamish. Finn bounces and flips and

leaps...until a disaster strikes. Hamish is left without a present. When Finn goes missing, Hamish frantically searches for him, unaware that at that very moment Finn is plotting the perfect solution...

ANNA WILSON BOOKS,
ILLUSTRATED BY MOIRA MUNRO

Look out for Anna Wilson's fun
series of Puppy, Kitten and other
books, all illustrated by Moira Munro,
and published by Macmillan. Here are a
few of them.

MORE BOOKS WRITTEN OR
ILLUSTRATED BY MOIRA MUNRO

For more of the latest books, visit

Moira Munro's website:

www.moiramunro.com

'The Mermaid who Came to School'
is also available as a colour paperback
(ISBN 978-1468060232), as an
audiobook, and as an ebook in a variety
of formats.

Printed in Great Britain
by Amazon.co.uk, Ltd.,
Marston Gate.